Dasher
Gets Adopted

A story of love, trust, and family.

By Julie Hatley

Illustrated by Shay Jones

~~~

Shine Publications

"Dasher Gets Adopted" is a work of fiction.

"Dasher Gets Adopted" is published by Shine Publications.
All rights reserved.
ISBN 0-9705188-0-3

Copyright 2001 by Julie Hatley

Shine Publications
PO Box 318
Issaquah, WA 98027-0013
www.shinepublications.com

First Edition.

Library of Congress Card Number: 00-192708

Printed in the United States of America.

For Brian.

And for Candy.

Dasher lived at the greyhound racing park.

Her favorite thing to do was running around the circular track. She also liked being with all her friends.

One day, Dasher learned she was being adopted and would be moving away from the race track.

She was scared when Georgia and John, her new owners, lead her to their car.

In the backseat, Dasher met Bobby, Georgia and John's little boy.

They kept looking at her and smiling. Dasher thought they must be taking her to another dog racing track.

Dasher squeezed in next to Bobby.
The car's swaying and turning made
her stomach queasy.

She put her head down and napped,
thinking everything would be just as it
had been before.

After a while the car stopped, and Dasher was happy to get out and stretch her long legs.

After a quick shake from head to tail, she was ready to see her greyhound friends.

Georgia and John invited Dasher into a building that looked nothing like the dog track.

She had expected to see kennel beds and dogs, but there were tables, chairs, and unfamiliar items instead.

Dasher sniffed, but couldn't smell anything familiar. She listened, but couldn't hear any barking.

She looked around, but didn't see any of her friends.

Dasher trembled with disappointment and fear. Why had she moved here? Had she done something bad?

Bobby, smiling and talking nonstop, walked her around the house.

When they came upon the stairwell, Dasher froze and stared way up. She had never climbed so many stairs at the dog track.

They placed Dasher's paws on the steps as they went. By the time they reached the top, Dasher was doing it on her own. Stairs weren't so hard after all!

They walked around the bedroom and Dasher was told this was where she would sleep.

Dasher looked at the big, soft bed in the center of the room, and hopped right on top!

"This is your bed, Dasher," Bobby said, pointing at the dog bed on the floor. Dasher jumped down as she was told.

She was sorry for her mistake, and decided to investigate her bed by the window.

Bonk! went Dasher's nose into the clear glass. She yelped in surprise.

"You've never seen a window before, have you?" John asked as he checked Dasher's hurt nose.

Dasher backed quickly away and rammed into a table with a thud!

A lamp tipped and fell over. "Be careful Dasher," they said.

Feeling much better downstairs again, Dasher wondered when she would be let outside?

Her potty trips at the race track had been scheduled, and she didn't know how to tell them that she had to go!

"No, Dasher!" cried John when he saw the puddle on the carpet.

Dasher knew she'd made another mistake. She had made so many. Was he going to punish her?

Dasher feared what John might do, and backed away from him.

An open door signaled her way to escape. She darted through in a hurry!

Georgia, John, and Bobby gave chase in a panic! Dasher wasn't safe running loose without a leash.

Could they keep her from getting hurt? Would they catch the fast dog in time?

Dasher reached full speed in three easy strides.

Ears raked back, neck stretched forward, Dasher's strong muscles carried her further and further away.

Houses and trees became streets and
moving cars as Dasher blindly fled.

A loud piercing squeal stopped Dasher in
her tracks. She watched in terror as a car
swerved to miss her!

Shocked and confused, Dasher didn't notice when they had finally caught up with her.

They slipped the leash over her head, and hugged and kissed her all the way home.

Exhausted, Dasher fell into a troubled sleep.

Why had she moved here? She remembered she hadn't won her last race. Was that what she had done wrong?

As time went on, Dasher started to enjoy their sweet praises, comforting hugs, and kind patience.

She slowly came to trust and like them.

Dasher's confidence grew, and so did her antics. She tossed her stuffed toys, and playbowed Bobby.

They laughed even when she tried to get them to play at midnight!

Overcoming her fear of going outside
again wasn't easy, but Dasher soon
loved taking walks in the neighborhood.

Fluttering leaves and scampering
squirrels made each trip a fun adventure.

Dasher often begged to go to the fenced field at the park where she could run and play safely.

Buzzing past Bobby at full speed was such a delight!

Dasher was thrilled to have her own private racing area in the backyard.

Sailing over flower beds and dodging bushes was much more fun than running circles at the race track!

One day, they kissed Dasher goodbye and said they had to leave her alone while they went to work.

Dasher didn't pay much attention until she woke up from her nap and realized she was alone.

Dasher watched out the window for them. She paced and panted with worry.

Were Georgia, John, and Bobby ever coming back?

Just when it was getting dark and Dasher's hope had almost run out, she saw their car pull into the driveway.

She was so happy to see them that she barked loudly, wagged wildly, and jumped for joy!

Suddenly, Dasher knew she had moved here so they would be a family, and love each other.

Dasher realized she was a very lucky greyhound, and that adoption was a good thing.

Give the Gift of Love, Trust, and Family to Your Friends and Loved Ones.

"Dasher Gets Adopted"

Contact your leading bookseller, or order here.

Please send me _____ copies of "Dasher Gets Adopted" at $14.95 each, plus $3.50 S&H per book. Washington residents please add $1.30 sales tax per book.

Canadian orders are welcome with a postal money order in U.S. funds. Please double the postage amount.

Allow 2 weeks for delivery.
www.shinepublications.com

Name _____

Organization _____

Address _____

City, State, Zip _____

Phone # _____ Email _____

Visa/MC # (circle) _____

Exp. Date _____ Exact Name on Card _____

Please make your check or money order payable to Shine Publications. Mail to:
Shine Publications
PO Box 318
Issaquah, WA 98027-0013

Phone: 425-254-0030   Fax: 425-254-9742